TRACKING *CHAMP*

STONE ARCH BOOKS
a capstone imprint

SNOOPS, INC. IS PUBLISHED BY
STONE ARCH BOOKS, A CAPSTONE IMPRINT
1710 ROE CREST DRIVE
NORTH MANKATO, MINNESOTA 56003
WWW.MYCAPSTONE.COM

Library of Congress Cataloging-in-Publication Data
Names: Terrell, Brandon, 1978– author. | Epelbaum, Mariano, 1975– illustrator.
Title: Tracking Champ / by Brandon Terrell ; illustrated by Mariano Epelbaum.
Description: North Mankato, Minnesota : Stone Arch Books, a Capstone imprint,
[2017] | Series: Snoops, Inc.
Identifiers: LCCN 2016033025 (print) | LCCN 2016035074 (ebook) |
ISBN 9781496543486 (library binding) | ISBN 9781496543523 (paperback) |
ISBN 9781496543646 (eBook PDF)
Subjects: LCSH: Mascots—Juvenile fiction. | Dogs—Juvenile fiction. |
Hispanic American boys—Juvenile fiction. | Twins—Juvenile fiction. |
Brothers and sisters—Juvenile fiction. | African American girls—Juvenile
fiction. | Friendship—Juvenile fiction. | Detective and mystery stories. |
CYAC: Mystery and detective stories. | Mascots—Fiction. | Dogs—Fiction. |
Hispanic Americans—Fiction. | Twins—Fiction. | Brothers and sisters—Fiction.
| African Americans—Fiction. | Friendship—Fiction. | GSAFD: Mystery fiction.
| LCGFT: Detective and mystery fiction.
Classification: LCC PZ7.T273 Tr 2017 (print) | LCC PZ7.T273 (ebook) |
DDC 813.6 [Fic]—dc23
LC record available at https://lccn.loc.gov/2016033025

BY BRANDON TERRELL

**ILLUSTRATED BY
MARIANO EPELBAUM**

EDITED BY: AARON SAUTTER
BOOK DESIGN BY: TED WILLIAMS
PRODUCTION BY: STEVE WALKER

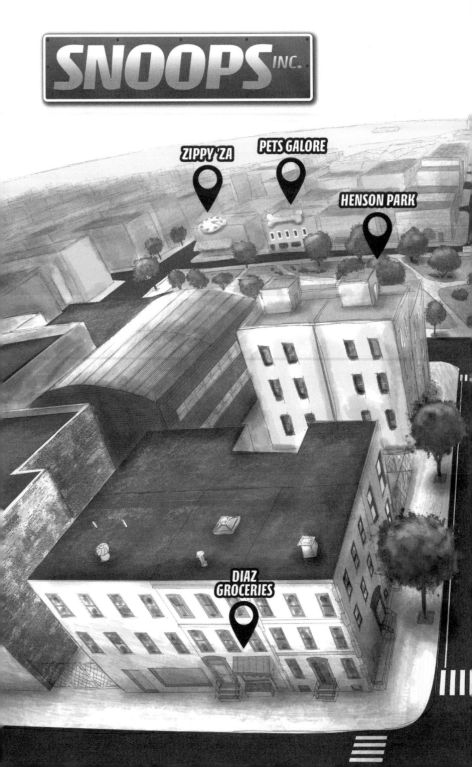

CHAPTER 1

STOP! THIEF!

It was growing dark as the girl walked down the sidewalk alone. Around her the city's tall buildings stood clustered together, stretching up toward the clouds. The sun had dropped below the skyline. Shadows grew long and dark as the street's lights came to life. The girl walked in and out of the pools of light as she focused on the task at hand. She wasn't afraid, though. She was never afraid.

The girl wore a pink hooded sweatshirt and carried a large, colorful purse over one shoulder. The purse stood out like a beacon in the streetlight. That was good. It was supposed to stand out. That's why she'd picked it from all the others in her closet.

From her left, down an alley, there was a flicker of movement. A shadowy figure slunk forward and began to follow the girl. She could sense him. At first, he was quiet, but after a block, he wasn't even trying to mask his footsteps.

As the girl stepped out of a pool of light, the figure rushed forward. He plucked the purse from the girl's arm, like a bird snatching prey off the ground, and took off running.

The girl, thirteen-year-old Keisha Turner, didn't even protest. She watched the man run down the block. "He's got it," Keisha said, appearing to speak to no one. "Hayden, is the tracking device working?"

An excited voice responded on the headset hidden beneath the tight brown curls of Keisha's hair. "It sure is!"

"Your plan worked," Keisha said. "This guy's purse-grabbing days are over."

"That's for sure. He messed with the wrong detectives," twelve-year-old Hayden Williams said. Then, after a moment of silence, she added, "He's running down Eleventh Avenue now, about to reach the intersection."

"I'm on it!" the voice of Jaden Williams, Hayden's over-eager twin brother, piped up over the headset.

Jaden pedaled his bike furiously down Greenhill Street, toward Eleventh Avenue. He had his baseball cap pulled low, and the wind cut across his face as he zipped down the street. He passed a diner with delicious smells that made him want to take a detour. He felt his stomach rumble. He would love to devour a juicy cheeseburger and a mountain of French fries right now.

"The job comes first," he muttered. His stomach grumbled an angry reply. "Sorry, buddy."

Up ahead, Jaden saw the purse snatcher jogging through the intersection. He wasn't moving as fast as before; he thought he was in the clear. The man was tall and wiry, and looked out of place carrying the colorful bag. He turned and headed straight toward Jaden.

Jaden squeezed his brakes and brought his bike to a stuttering stop right in front of the purse snatcher. "Hey!" the man called out. He stumbled back.

"Nice purse you have there," Jaden said. "The color really brings out your eyes."

The man, realizing that something was up, spun and dashed down a nearby alleyway.

"Just where I want you," Jaden said. He pressed a button on his phone. "He's in the alleyway on Eleventh, heading south."

The alley was narrow. The heat of the day was trapped inside, making it hot. It smelled like spoiled garbage. There were no fire escapes, no places to climb. A small space between the brick buildings at the other end was the only way out.

The purse snatcher ran toward the end of the alley. He was almost to freedom, and —

"Oof!"

A strong leg shot out from behind a dumpster on the left. As the thief tripped, he let go of the purse to break his fall with both hands. The purse sailed through the air and landed a few feet away as the thief landed hard on the asphalt.

A teenage boy, fourteen-year-old Carlos Diaz, scooped up the fallen purse. He smiled mischievously. "I believe this belongs to my friend," Carlos said.

The purse snatcher rolled onto his back, trying to catch his breath.

Carlos unzipped the purse and pulled out a sleek black device with a blinking red light.

"My friends are crazy smart," Carlos said. "They whipped up this fancy tracking device, and we used it to follow you. Pretty cool, huh?"

The purse snatcher moaned in protest, but remained on the ground.

Carlos saw Jaden, still on his bike, at the far end of the alley. Hayden stood beside him now, holding her electronic tablet and wearing a set of headphones.

Keisha jogged up behind Carlos. "Good work, Carlos," she said.

"Thanks," he said. "You call the police?"

"You know it."

As if on cue, red and blue police lights appeared. The cars' lights and sirens bounced around the alley like a pinball in a machine.

"Congratulations," Carlos said to the purse snatcher, "you've just been busted by Snoops, Inc."

CHAPTER 2

A NEW CHAMP

"Attention all students," Principal Snider's voice boomed over the PA system at Fleischman Middle School the following afternoon. "Today's pep rally to celebrate our boys' basketball team begins in ten minutes."

Carlos stared up at the speaker from his desk. A couple of other kids in his eighth-grade geography class whooped and cheered. "Go Bulldogs!" yelled Amelia Thornton. She was part of the spirit squad. In response, two other students growled like hungry dogs in need of kibble.

Carlos rolled his eyes.

"Today we'll have a very special guest at the rally," Principal Snider continued. "So hurry on down! You are now free to leave class and head directly to the gymnasium."

Students leaped to their feet and shuffled toward the door. Carlos shoved his books into his backpack and joined them.

The school hallways were covered in colorful banners and signs. Glittery, block letters spelled out slogans like "BULLDOGS R #1" and "GO BULLDOGS GO! RUFF RUFF!" The halls were buzzing with activity. Carlos felt like he'd been caught in a roaring river as he joined the flood of students moving toward the gym.

"Carlos!" Keisha yelled from her locker at the edge of the crowd. Carlos peered past the other kids in the hall to see her waving.

"Wait up!" Keisha shouted.

"Can't!" Carlos shouted back. "I'll get trampled if I alter course!"

Keisha dove into the flow, making her way toward him. Unlike Carlos, the seventh grader had no problem throwing elbows and fighting to keep her place. "Hey," she said calmly as she sidled up next to him. She seemed oblivious to the seventh grader who she'd just nudged out of her way.

Together, the two friends walked to the gym. As they reached it, they could hear the booming Bulldog pep band playing the school fight song. A group of spirit squad members stood near the door, waving their red and brown pom-poms and greeting their friends with bubbly hellos.

One of the squad members, a pretty girl with shoulder-length black hair named Frankie Dixon, frowned when she saw Carlos and Keisha drawing near.

"'Sup, Frankie," Carlos said. He tried to flash his usual charm, but it had no effect on Frankie.

She said nothing. Instead, she just gave Keisha a sour, lingering stare, then turned her back on them.

Carlos said nothing. Once upon a time, Keisha and Frankie had been BFFs. Like, the B-est of Fs. But then something happened between them, something Keisha never revealed to any of them. She only referred to it as The Fallout. Whatever it was, The Fallout caused a rift in their friendship. The two girls had barely spoken since.

Fleischman was an old school, made of cracked brick and stone. The wooden bleachers and hardwood gym floor hadn't been changed since the school opened almost a century ago. Carlos spotted Hayden and Jaden sitting together near the other sixth graders. Jaden nodded his head at Carlos; the elder Snoop nodded back. Then he and Keisha found an open seat next to their friends and sat.

A podium had been set up under one of the basketball hoops alongside a row of metal folding chairs. Principal Snider, a thickset man whose bald head glinted in the gym lights, stood behind the podium.

When the pep band finished, Principal
Snider stepped up to the podium's microphone.
"Ahem." His throat-clearing echoed through
the gym. "What an exciting time for Fleischman
Middle School. As you know, this Friday evening,
our boys' basketball team faces off against our
rivals, the Watson Hurricanes —"

A thundering chorus of "Boos!" interrupted
Principal Snider. He waved both hands to silence
the students, then continued. "All right, all right.
I like your passion, but let's turn those boos to
cheers. Join me in welcoming the Fleischman
Fighting Bulldogs boys' basketball team!"

The crowd rose to its feet as a line of boys
entered the gym. The head of the line was led by
a handsome jock named Ashton Oakley. He was
the kind of kid who would probably never have
to deal with acne or braces. The kind who skated
by on popularity. The kind Carlos had absolutely
zero time for.

Flanked by members of the spirit squad, the
basketball team made their way to the line of

chairs. They all sat except for Ashton. The star athlete remained standing alongside Principal Snider. "We're all very excited about the game this Friday, Ashton," the principal said.

"Thanks," Ashton said. "And we're excited to kick Watson's butt!"

This drew another round of cheers and barks from the crowd. When they'd dwindled, Principal Snider said, "Now, about that very special guest we have. Would you all like to meet him?"

The crowd cheered.

"Good!" Principal Snider waved to someone hidden just out of Carlos' sight at the end of the bleachers. "We here at Fleischman have been searching for the perfect team mascot. Today, we're officially introducing him to the school. Boys and girls, I give you . . . Champ!"

A big, slobbering bulldog on a leash tottered quickly into the gym. He was brown with white patches. A thick, bright-red collar hung around his neck. Champ's long tongue flopped out of his mouth as he bounded around the basketball court. The cheering crowd only made Champ more frantic. It seemed to Carlos like the bulldog fed off the attention.

Champ's leash was being barely held by Polly McDonald, Principal Snider's student assistant. She wrangled the crazed bulldog to the podium and passed the leash to Principal Snider.

"What do you think?!" Principal Snider knelt by Champ, who promptly licked the principal on the cheeks and face. He scratched the scruff behind Champ's ear. "Who's a good doggie?"

Ashton Oakley, still standing at the podium, said, "I think we all love Champ!"

The students hollered and whistled their agreement.

Ashton continued. "Now let's show our new mascot how we play basketba– basket– ah– CHOO!" The jock let loose a mighty sneeze and the microphone screeched with feedback.

Principal Snider stood. "Uh-oh," he joked, clapping Ashton on the back. "I hope you're not getting sick before the big game."

Ashton smiled. "Not a chance, sir," he said.

"Then why don't you lead us all in a lively singing of our school fight song?" Principal Snider passed Champ's leash back to Polly as Ashton began to sing. The whole student body joined in. The pep band played loud and proud. The gym was filled with music and the barking of the Fleischman Fighting Bulldogs' brand new mascot.

● ● ●

The remainder of the school day, all anyone could talk about was Champ. The bulldog was an instant hit. The lovable mutt sat for photos with anyone who wanted one, including Keisha, who made Carlos wait for her while she snapped a selfie with the pup. Then Polly needed to take him back to his kennel in the school courtyard. Champ was the school mascot, but was also Principle Snider's new family pet. The lovable mutt stayed in the large metal kennel during the school day.

In every one of Carlos' afternoon classes, students raved about Champ. When the final bell rang, Carlos headed to the school's big front doors. He bounded down the stone steps to the bike rack, where his BMX was locked. He'd just begun to pedal away when he felt a familiar buzz in his pocket and heard its corresponding chirp.

Gliding down the sidewalk, Carlos drew his phone from his pocket. When he read the text from Keisha, though, he slammed on the brakes.

The text read:

CHAMP IS MISSING!!!

CHAPTER 3

ON THE CASE

Looks like Snoops, Inc., has a new case to solve, Carlos thought as he swung his bike around and headed back to school.

Keisha was waiting for him outside the principal's office, arms folded across her chest. The office door was closed. He could see Principal

Snider pacing and talking to Polly McDonald through the narrow, vertical window.

"What happened?" Carlos asked. He'd instantly gone into detective mode.

Keisha shrugged. "Polly just came running through here in tears," she said. "Champ's kennel door was open, and he's nowhere to be found."

"Do you think we can take a look at the kennel?" Carlos asked.

"Let's do it."

The small courtyard was located in the middle of the school. It was mostly made of cement, but there was a patch of grass and a tree offering shade along one wall of the school. Picnic tables had been set up under the tree. A chain-link fence blocked off the other side of the courtyard, which opened onto the street and the city beyond it.

"That gate is usually closed," Keisha noted, pointing at the fence. The chained gate was open by a few feet.

"The gap is wide enough for Champ to squeeze through," Carlos said. He had his phone out and began to snap photos of the scene. They were both careful not to touch anything.

Keisha was investigating the metal dog kennel. It was set against the brick wall of the school, right next to the window of Principal Snider's office. The kennel stood about five feet tall and was just as wide. A lumpy, plaid pillow sat in one corner, along with a chewed up, oversized plastic bone and two red dishes. One was filled with food, the other with water.

"The door to the kennel has a latch," Keisha noted as Carlos snapped a photo of it. "There's no way Champ could unlock it on his own."

"Unless he's got mad doggie skills," Carlos said. *Click.* He took a photo of the latch.

"Or if someone forgot to lock it." Keisha crouched down and peered inside the kennel. Carlos joined her, taking photos of Champ's doggie dishes and his pillow, which was covered in short, brown dog hair.

"Excuse me. What do you think you're doing?" Principal Snider's stern voice shot goosebumps up

and down Carlos' arms and spine. It wasn't the first time he and the other Snoops had earned the principal's attention, but Carlos hated getting in trouble. He stood and stashed his phone in his pocket, then faced the principal. Snider was not alone; Polly McDonald was behind him, lost in his massive shadow.

"Diaz and Turner," Principal Snider said. "I should have known I'd find you two snooping around out here."

"It's what we do best," Carlos said, flashing his most honest smile.

"Champ's escape is awful," Keisha said. "We just hope we can find him."

Principal Snider shifted his weight from one foot to the other and crossed his arms. He stared down his nose at the kids, then grunted. "Awful is right," Principal Snider said. "I just adopted Champ last week, and he's already become a wonderful pet for my family. I can't imagine the poor guy out there, loose in the city. All because of a silly unlatched kennel."

He sighed. "All right. I'll take all the extra eyes searching for him that I can. I've already begun making flyers to help find Champ. Students who wish to post them around the neighborhood can find them in my office tomorrow after class. Carry on." He turned on his heel and strode back into the school.

Polly McDonald remained. She had her hands clasped together and was staring at Champ's kennel. Her eyes were red and puffy, but the tears had stopped.

"Polly?" Carlos asked. "Are you all right?"

"He . . . he blames me," she said quietly.

"Who blames you?" Keisha asked.

"Principal Snider. He blames me for Champ's disappearance. I . . . I . . ." Tears began to fill Polly's eyes again and then slip down her cheeks.

They waited in silence as Polly blew her nose into a tissue, then took a deep breath.

When Polly had composed herself, she said, "I'm so sorry."

"Hey, it's okay," Carlos said. He dug into his pocket and pulled out a business card. On it was an image of a magnifying glass along with the words:

Snoops, Incorporated
No case too small . . .
we solve them all!

An address was listed below it, along with Carlos' cell phone number and email address.

"Here," he said. "Take your time, collect yourself, and visit us later. Sound good?"

Polly nodded. She sniffled and took the business card. Then she slipped silently toward the school door.

• • •

The headquarters for Snoops, Incorporated, was in the basement of the apartment building where the four young detectives lived. Rows of chain-link fence storage lockers stood throughout the basement. Most were filled with junk, holiday decorations, old clothes, and books.

The Snoops team had gotten permission to convert an extra storage locker into an office space. It included a wooden desk and chairs, a lamp, and a dusty old filing cabinet.

"Nothing looks out of the ordinary in these photos, aside from the gate being open," Keisha said. She and Carlos were seated at the desk. They'd transferred the photos they'd taken earlier onto the old, clunky desktop computer that Keisha's mom had given them. The computer's fan wheezed as they sorted and clicked through the images.

"Poor Champ," Hayden said. She sat on the floor, fingers flying across her tablet. A giant grape sucker made her left cheek bulge outward and her words muffled. "Out roaming the city by himself." She reached over to pet Agatha, the stray orange tabby cat who visited Snoops HQ daily and who was currently curled up and sleeping beside her.

"And poor Principal Snider," Carlos added. "He must feel awful about losing his family's new pet."

"I bet someone found him and is taking care of him." Jaden was lounging in the office's lumpy armchair, flipping through an issue of *Ninja Mummy*, his favorite comic book. "He's probably living large right now in a high-rise, taking a bulldog bubble bath."

"I hope so," Hayden said. "I'm gonna see if anybody at the YFC has any suggestions." Hayden was part of an online group called the Young Forensics Club. She and a number of kids discussed crimes and detection techniques with one another. The YFC had been helpful to the Snoops before, and Hayden often bragged about their investigative achievements on the site.

"Hello?" a timid voice called out, followed by the sound of shuffling feet. "Carlos?"

Jaden quickly sat up and tucked his comic away. "You hear that?" he asked, taking off his baseball hat and smoothing his hair. Then he crammed the hat back onto his head. "We've got a customer."

"We're back here," Carlos called out. His voice echoed off the cement walls.

A moment later, Polly McDonald appeared in the hall outside the Snoops office. She looked around, hesitant and nervous-looking. Crumpled in her hands was a used tissue.

"Come in," Carlos said. Jaden quickly leaped up and offered Polly his seat.

"Thanks." Polly blew her nose into the tissue, a loud honking sound that surprised Jaden and made him step back.

Carlos leaned on the desk and crossed his arms as Polly sat in the offered chair. "So how are you feeling?" he asked.

"Better," Polly said.

"Any word on Champ yet?" Keisha asked
She shook her head.

"Can you tell us what happened today?" Carlos asked gently.

"I . . . I took Champ out for a walk," Polly explained. "He was riled up after the assembly. We went around the block a couple of times. Then I kenneled him and went back to class. After school, when I went to check on him, he was . . ."

She trailed off.

"And the gate was open? Like this?" Keisha asked, swinging the old desktop computer's dusty screen around and showing Polly one of Carlos' photos.

Polly nodded. "I swear I latched it, though," she said. She pointed at the open latch, a pin dangling free on a small chain. "I like to be organized, and I know I latched it. I double checked it before I left."

"You're sure?" Carlos asked gently. He didn't want to upset her further.

Polly scrunched up her face. "I must have . . . I . . ." She thought a moment. "I had a test in American History, and I was running late. But I swear. I'm a responsible person . . ." She took a deep breath to compose herself, then said,

"Principal Snider thinks I forgot to lock it. He doesn't believe me at all."

"Well, we believe you," Carlos said, glancing at the other Snoops. They all nodded. "If you say you locked it, then that means someone came around and unlocked it. Champ's been dognapped, and we're going to find him."

"We promise," Jaden added.

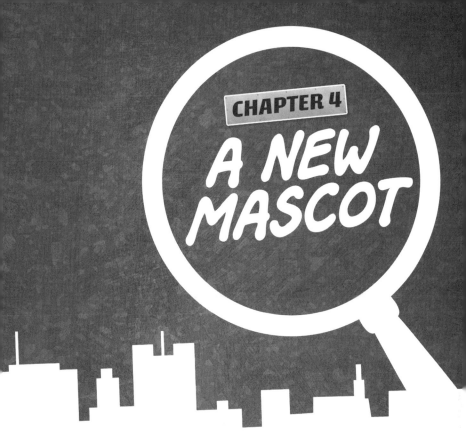

CHAPTER 4

A NEW MASCOT

"Dognapped." Jaden shook his head. "You really think someone took Champ?"

"I don't know," Carlos said. "But if Polly's telling the truth, and she really did latch the kennel, then someone stole our new mascot."

"Who would do something like that?" Keisha sounded disgusted.

It was the following morning, and the four Snoops were walking to school. Jaden lazily wove his skateboard around pedestrians and hopped off curbs.

"The real question is why," Carlos said. "That'll lead us to who."

"What if it's a prank?" Hayden's fingers danced across the tablet cradled in the crook of one arm. "With the big basketball game coming up, it could have easily been someone from Watson Middle School who took Champ. They have a history of pranking our teams." She showed them the tablet screen, which displayed an article about Watson athletes sticking plastic forks into the Fleischman football field the night before Homecoming.

"Good call," Carlos said.

"So we should talk to the basketball team," Jaden said.

"Remember, Principal Snider is printing flyers in the office today," Keisha said. "We should pick some up after school."

"Good idea," Carlos said. "I can put them up in my dad's store." Carlos' dad ran Diaz Groceries, a small shop across the street from their apartment building.

"Meet in the cafeteria after school?" Keisha asked.

"Cool," Carlos said. "Sounds like a plan."

* * *

"Oh, man, I can't believe I get to meet Ashton Oakley," Jaden said as he and Carlos walked into the gymnasium after school. "He's, like, the best basketball player in the state."

"Just don't fanboy out too much," Carlos said. "Remember, we're trying to solve a mystery here."

"Right." Then, under his breath, Jaden added, "Keep it together, man. Keep it together."

Squeaking sneakers and bouncing basketballs created a strange, off-beat rhythm in the school's gymnasium. A few team members were already practicing, but most sat courtside on the first row of bleachers. Coach Buxton, a towering man with a goatee and a Bulldogs B-Ball T-shirt, stood under the hoop grabbing rebounds, but practice hadn't officially started.

Carlos spied Ashton Oakley seated on the bleachers, lacing up his sneakers.

"Hey, guys," Carlos said as he and Jaden approached.

Ashton looked up in a way that basically said, *Who are you, and what do you want?*

"Total bummer about Champ running away, huh?" Carlos began.

Ashton shrugged. "Yeah, I guess."

"Makes you wonder if maybe someone from Watson took our mascot," Carlos prodded.

"Huh. Actually, I heard that quiet girl left his kennel unlocked," Ashton said.

"So Watson hasn't joked about the missing mascot yet?" Jaden asked.

Ashton shook his head. "Nothin' about Champ. Just the usual 'we're gonna get you' garbage on School Ties."

School Ties was a website used by area middle and high schools as a place for students to chat. Or, in this case, to trash talk the opposing team.

"Gotcha. Let me know if they do?" Carlos asked.

"Can do," Ashton replied.

From across the gym, Carlos heard the spirit squad squeal. "Oh, it looks so good!" one girl shouted.

"It's perfect, Frankie!" said another.

Carlos turned to see the team near the far bleachers. They weren't alone, though. A person in a gigantic bulldog costume waved his arms and flexed. The bulldog wore a Fleischman basketball jersey and was surrounded by spirit squad members.

"What's going on?" Carlos muttered.

Frankie Dixon stood beside the mascot, arms crossed, smiling smugly.

"Oh, that's Chomp," Ashton said.

Carlos was puzzled. "Chomp?"

"I guess Frankie's dad heard about us not having a mascot for the game anymore," Ashton explained. "So he went ahead and bought the Chomp outfit. You know, to cheer us up."

Chomp danced around with the spirit squad girls. He shook his tail right in Frankie's face. She swatted it away and giggled.

"But we already have a mascot," Jaden said.

A wide smile flashed across Ashton's face. "Looking good, Chomp!" he shouted across the gym, flashing a thumbs-up.

Chomp waved back frenetically with both hands at the basketball team. Other players whooped and cheered.

"Excuse me," said a voice behind Carlos. A lean boy with a shock of spiky brown hair breezed past the two Snoops. Carlos recognized him from class; his name was Oliver Noonan.

Oliver sat on the bleacher beside Ashton. He dropped his backpack and shed his coat in a flurry of motion.

"You're late, Ollie!" Coach Buxton said.

"Sorry, Coach," Ollie replied, fumbling with his sneakers.

"Gotta be on time to ride that pine," Ashton joked, playfully shoving Ollie and chuckling.

Ollie smiled. "Exactly," he said. It seemed like he was in on the joke, but Carlos could see a glimmer of frustration in Ollie's eyes.

He knew how the kid felt. He'd really been banking on the b-ball team to give him info that would send the Snoops in the right direction.

"Looks like practice is about to start," Carlos said. "Remember, if you hear anything from Watson, let us know, okay?" He passed Ashton a business card.

"Yeah, sure," Ashton said. The athlete tossed Ollie's coat off his gym bag. He quickly stashed the card inside the bag and slung it over his shoulder.

Suddenly the star athlete's nose twitched once, twice . . . and then he unleashed a wild sneeze.

"Ah-CHOO!"

Jaden, who'd been starstruck the whole time, whispered, "*Gesundheit.*" Then he added, "Um . . . can I have your autograph?"

Ashton sniffled, then gave him a weird look. "You kidding me?"

Jaden laughed nervously. "Ha. Yeah. Totally kidding. I'm . . . I'm leaving now." He hustled across the gym, his cheeks bright red.

Carlos snickered to himself about Jaden before following him out of the gym. As he left, he pondered what he learned during his brief talk with Ashton.

• • •

The two boys met Keisha and Hayden a short time later in the cafeteria. The four Snoops sat at a round table to talk. Jaden munched on an apple he'd discovered in his backpack. How long it had been in there was a mystery even Snoops, Inc., couldn't solve.

"Frankie's dad bought a bulldog costume?" Keisha's face was twisted in confusion.

"I guess," Carlos said. "Name's Chomp."

"Geez," Hayden said. "Champ has barely been gone a day. Tacky much?"

"That's Frankie's style," Keisha muttered. "Did the team know anything about Champ?"

Carlos shook his head. "Just some trash-talking about the game on School Ties," he said. "Hayden, can you keep tabs on Watson's page, see if anything about Champ pops up?"

"On it," Hayden said. She immediately slid her tablet out of her backpack and jumped online. She quickly set up an alert for any mention of Champ's name on the site.

When she'd confirmed that there was no new info about Champ, the detectives gathered their things and walked to Principal Snider's office to pick up flyers. As they approached, Carlos noticed a swarm of kids near the principal's office.

"I can't believe how many people are here to help find Champ," Hayden said.

"Agreed," Keisha said. She lowered her head and nudged past a trio of spirit squad girls who were passing flyers to one another.

"Keisha, watch out!" Carlos tried to grab her, but was a step too far behind. With her head down,

down, Keisha didn't notice the last spirit squad girl to exit the office.

Thud!

Keisha slammed into the girl, and a spray of flyers fluttered to the floor.

"Oh, that's just perfect," Frankie Dixon said. "Thanks a lot."

"Sorry," Keisha mumbled in a tone that bordered on fake.

Frankie bent down to scoop up the scattered paper. "Whatever." She adjusted her skirt. "I suppose you and your . . . friends think you're going to find Champ?"

Hayden nodded. "We will."

Carlos glanced around. "So where's your spirit squad's new pal, Chomp?" he joked.

Frankie put a hand on her hip. "If it were up to me, we wouldn't have had a stinky dog as a mascot anyway. The spirit squad wanted a bulldog costume, but Principal Snider said a real one would be more fun. Ashton Oakley thinks the new mascot is a great idea. He loves Chomp."

Then Frankie breezed away, joining her spirit squad comrades. They began to tape the flyers wherever they could find space in the halls.

"Well, that was . . . pleasant," Hayden said.

Carlos watched Frankie, then looked over at Keisha. Without a word, he knew they were thinking the same thing: *We just found our first suspect.*

But as crazy as Frankie Dixon could be, would she really dognap Champ just because she'd rather have someone in a mascot costume?

"Come on," Keisha said, leading the way into Principal Snider's office. A number of students were still milling about. Polly McDonald appeared overwhelmed, so the look she gave when she saw Keisha was one of pure relief.

"Any update?" Polly asked.

Carlos shook his head. "Nothing yet," he said. "We were hoping to score some flyers, though."

"Here." Polly handed him a large stack of flyers. On them, Champ's slobbery, adorable face stared back at him. His tongue lolled out of his mouth, and his underbite jutted out, exposing his teeth. His bright-red collar was the only pop of color on the drab flyers, which had the school's phone number listed below the words LOST DOG.

"Please find him," Polly said. "I couldn't sleep at all last night. I kept thinking of poor Champ, how I was the last person to see Principal Snider's dog."

"Thanks," Carlos said. "We'll be in touch."

The Snoops set off down the hall with a handful of flyers, a new suspect, and a whole new set of questions to answer.

CHAPTER 5

PETS GALORE

"Frankie Dixon? A suspect?" Jaden asked when the four Snoops were outside the school. "I don't believe it. You really think the spirit squad would dognap Champ as a form of protest?"

"Doesn't seem like something she'd do," Hayden added.

"Once upon a time, I'd agree," Keisha said. "But now . . . well, I don't know what to think."

"Well, I think there's one obvious place we haven't checked yet," Carlos said. "The closest pet store is also an animal shelter. Pets Galore. If someone found Champ, there's a good chance he'd be there."

"That's right! Let's check it out," Jaden said, dropping his skateboard and hopping on.

The young sleuths hustled through the city streets, down a few blocks, and through a small park. Carlos knew right where Pets Galore was located; his favorite pizza joint, Zippy 'Za, was right next door.

An orange awning hung out over a large window where six or seven puppies could be seen wrestling with one another. Above them hung a sign saying they were available to be adopted by loving families. Hayden plastered her face to the glass. "Aw," she said. "They're adorable! I just wanna squish 'em!"

Inside, the sound grew. Dogs barked. Cats meowed. Birds chirped. A row of small kennels lined one wall, while a section in the back offered ample space for dogs and cats in need of a good home. Fish tanks gurgled nearby, and there was even an aisle of chew toys and treats and a display of collars and leashes.

A woman with wispy white hair stood behind the store's counter, feeding a ferret a small dish of dry food. She wore a T-shirt that featured an illustration of a cat with a mustache wearing a top hat. It also had the words: I'm the Cat's Meow.

"Hello, hello!" the woman called out cheerfully. "I'm Trina. How can I help you kids this afternoon?"

"Hi," Carlos said as Keisha passed him a flyer. "Have you seen this missing dog?" He slid the flyer across the counter to the pet store owner.

Trina scrutinized it, then shook her head. "Sorry," she said. "I haven't had anyone bring in a stray bulldog."

Keisha peered back at the kennels of pets. "So how often do people bring in pets?"

Trina shrugged. "Almost every day. Some are like your friend here, strays or lost animals without

collars or homes. Others are animals — mostly cats
and dogs — that people buy and take home. But
then they realize they're allergic to the animals."

"Really?" Hayden asked.

"Unfortunately, yes." Trina slid the ferret back
into its cage. She took the flyer and posted it on
a corkboard behind the counter. "About fifteen
percent of people are allergic to cats and dogs.
Some people don't find out until they actually have
a pet. But I'll keep my eye out for your friend."

"Thanks." Carlos offered her a business card before the Snoops headed back out of the store.

"Another dead end," Jaden said as they walked back home. The sun was dipping behind the skyscrapers, casting the whole city in warm hues of orange and red.

• • •

When the kids reconvened at Snoops HQ after dinner, Hayden was alive with energy. "Guys!" she shouted. "Check it out."

She had her tablet open to the School Ties website. More specifically, to the page for Watson Middle School. She pointed at a small comment in a thread about the basketball game, and Carlos read it aloud.

"*That Fleischman team's going to freak out when they see what we're doing,*" Carlos read.

"Oh, man," Jaden said. "I knew Frankie was too nice to dognap Champ. It has to be Watson. They must be talking about stealing our mascot."

Carlos saw Keisha roll her eyes. Poor Jaden had a huge crush on Frankie, despite her complete lack of charm.

"Let's not get ahead of ourselves," Carlos said. "But yeah, it sounds like we can officially add Watson to the list of suspects."

Agatha leaped up on the desk, as if to see what the Snoops were up to. She meowed softly and snuggled up against Hayden, sniffing and licking her hands.

"She must smell the animals from the pet store," Hayden said. To Agatha, she added, "Don't worry, sweetie. I'd never replace you."

"Oh, here. I brought her some food," Carlos said. He handed Hayden a small plastic bag. Inside, wrapped in crinkly white paper, was part of a salmon fish filet from Diaz Groceries.

Agatha's ears perked up even more when she smelled the fish and saw Hayden unwrapping it. Hayden placed the fish on a plate and had barely set it on the cement floor before Agatha began chowing down.

Hayden sat cross-legged on the floor beside her. "All those poor stray animals like Agatha," she said.

"With no one to feed them and keep track of them," Keisha said.

Hayden suddenly sat up straight. "That's it!" she belted out, startling the other three Snoops. Jaden nearly dropped his can of root beer.

"What's *it*?" Jaden asked.

Hayden scrambled to her feet and grabbed her backpack. "I need my tablet and I need to talk to Polly," she said.

"Okay," Carlos said, giving up the chair behind the desk for Hayden to sit.

"Oh!" Hayden added as she plopped down. "And I need a grape sucker."

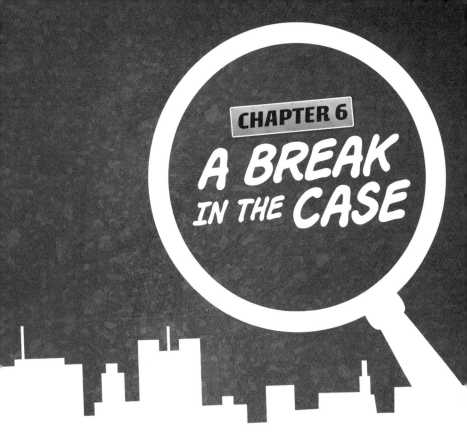

CHAPTER 6

A BREAK
IN THE CASE

Carlos watched Hayden swipe and type on her tablet. Agatha was curled up on the desk next to her; she scratched the cat behind its ear as she worked.

"So what's up?" Carlos asked.

"I may have a lead," Hayden said. "Just checking to see if any of my YFC friends can help us out."

"Polly's on her way," Keisha told her, thumbing her phone off. "She has the info you need."

"Cool," Hayden said. She looked up from the tablet and popped the ever-present grape sucker out of her mouth. "Look at the LOST DOG flyer," she said to the others. "And the selfie Keisha took with Champ yesterday."

Carlos flicked on the desktop computer and scrolled through to find the photo Keisha had taken with the bulldog. Both the girl and the dog had their tongues sticking out.

"Awww," Jaden joked. "Cute."

Keisha punched him on the shoulder. "Shut it," she said.

"Look, Champ's collar is from a brand called TechPet," Hayden explained. "I saw a bunch of them when we were at Pets Galore. Some of their models have trackers installed right in the collar."

"Kinda like injecting a microchip right under the pet's skin," Jaden said.

"Not exactly." Hayden went back to typing. "Microchips are for identification, in case the pet gets lost and brought in to a vet. These are collars that track an animal using GPS — global positioning satellites. Right now I'm trying to get info from any YFC member to a program called PetTracker3000. Oh, here we go."

As Hayden began her online conversation, Carlos heard the basement door groan open. A moment later, Polly appeared. She seemed more confident than the last time she'd visited.

"Hi, Polly," Carlos said. "Feeling better?"

"I am. Thanks." Polly held a small envelope in one hand. She passed it over to him. "Here's the info on Champ's collar. Principal Snider bought it from Pets Galore just last week."

"Did you know there was a tracking device on the collar?" Keisha asked.

Polly shook her head.

"Did Principal Snider?"

Another head shake.

"I'm in!" Hayden said. The kids crowded around her to get a good view. The sweet scent of Hayden's grape sucker filled the air.

On the tablet, a map of the city was displayed. In one corner was the logo for the PetTracker3000 app, a collar with wavy lines radiating out from it.

"Can I see the collar info?" Hayden asked. In all the excitement, Carlos had almost forgotten he was holding the envelope that Polly had brought.

"Oh," he said, passing it over. "Sorry."

Hayden tore open the envelope. Inside was a slip of paper with the TechPet logo and a string of numbers listed on the bottom.

"What are the odds our chip pops up at Watson Middle School?" Jaden asked.

"Or Frankie's penthouse," Keisha muttered. Her ex-friend's family was wealthy, and Frankie lived in a building with her dad's name on the side of it.

Hayden typed in the numbers and they waited. Finally, after a moment, a small red dot appeared in the middle of the map's grid.

"We've got him!" she shouted victoriously, waving her sucker over her head in triumph.

"Great job, Hayden," Carlos said.

"Thanks," she replied.

The red blip was located at neither of the places Keisha or Jaden suggested. In fact, Carlos wasn't sure exactly where Champ was on the map. He did know one thing, though.

"That's close," he said. "Maybe ten blocks, give or take."

He didn't have to tell Jaden twice. The young, headstrong Snoop was already halfway out of HQ. "Hurry!" he shouted. "Let's grab our bikes and solve this mystery once and for all!"

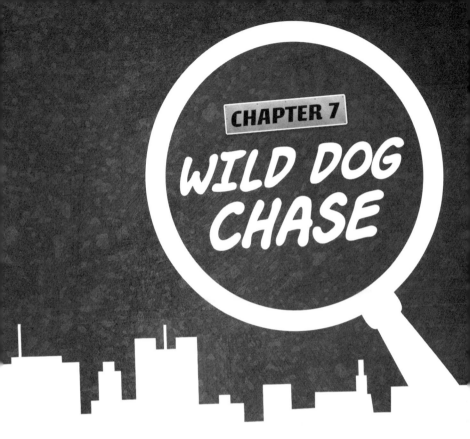

CHAPTER 7

WILD DOG CHASE

Dusk had not yet settled on the city. The Snoops sped along sidewalks and streets on their bikes. They pedaled as fast as they could, with Jaden in the lead and Hayden trailing behind the rest. Secured on a bracket between the bike's handlebars was her tablet. She kept an eye on the map on the screen as they rode along.

"Left at the next intersection!" Hayden
called out.

Jaden carved around the corner, narrowly
missing a street lamp that featured one of the
LOST DOG flyers Principal Snider had made. Carlos
followed, slower and more cautiously. Since Polly
had walked to Snoops HQ, she rode on his back
pegs, her hands clutching his shoulders tightly.

"Excuse us!" Carlos hollered. Up ahead on the
sidewalk, a group of pedestrians stood outside a
restaurant. They yelped and leaped aside as the
Snoops breezed past them.

"Watch it!" an older man bellowed after them.
Carlos turned back to see him waving a fist at
them. That was when he saw Hayden's glowing
face frown.

"What's up?" he asked.

"It's Champ," Hayden said. "He's on the move!"

The red dot had begun to slide along the grid,
further away from the Snoops. It was moving faster
than a dog could run. "He must be riding in a car,"
Carlos said when Hayden told them this info.

Hayden nodded. "We're going to lose him," she said.

"Then pedal faster!" Jaden shouted from the front of the pack. He bunny-hopped off the curb, onto a crosswalk, and through a green light.

The Snoops put on as much speed as they could. They even cut through a dark alleyway to try to catch up to the elusive moving dot. Carlos considered himself to be in shape, but his legs burned with each pump of the pedals.

Finally, Hayden said, "It's stopped! And we're getting close." The red dot hovered over an open block of land, right next to a park.

The Snoops stopped their bikes under a streetlight. Hayden studied the map, her nose nearly touching the tablet screen. "PetTracker says Champ should be somewhere in there."

She pointed to her left, at a spacious, fenced-in grassy area. A sign on the fence read: Ruff Patch Dog Park. A small parking lot held a number of cars, and tall trees surrounded the park.

"Look at that place," Jaden said. "It's sheer, slobbering chaos."

It was just around dinnertime, and a number of dogs frolicked in the park. Some owners chased after their dogs or threw Frisbees to them. Others just sat chatting with one another while their pets sniffed each other and rolled in the grass.

"According to the app, Champ is smack dab in the middle of that 'slobbery chaos,'" Hayden said. She swung her leg over her bike, leaned it against a tree, and began to walk toward the dog park.

Hayden didn't look where she was going. She had her eyes on her tablet, walking toward the middle of the dog park. Boxers and retrievers and wiener dogs circled around her. Some yipped, others sniffed. Normally, the pet-loving Hayden would be in heaven with all the doggie attention, but she was focused. She spun left, then back, then turned in a full circle.

"Champ . . . is . . . right . . ." She twirled and dramatically thrust out a finger. "There!"

Only, she wasn't pointing at a bulldog. She was pointing at a short dog with shaggy hair that hid his eyes. The dog was sitting on the grass, leisurely scratching itself behind one ear.

"What the . . . ?" Jaden said. "I know it's only been a day, but Champ looks . . . different."

"That's not Champ, dude," Carlos said.

"But that can't be right," Hayden said. She swiped at the app, quickly retyping the numerical code for Champ's collar into PetTracker3000. Again, the red blip appeared right in front of her.

The long-haired dog chuffed, then plopped onto its belly.

"Look." Keisha crouched down by the dog. She held out one hand, letting the animal sniff her to show she wasn't a threat. Then Keisha drew back some of the dog's scruffy hair to reveal a familiar bright-red collar. "This must be Champ's collar."

"Hey, what's up?" a voice drawled from behind them. "Is Killer okay?"

Carlos turned and saw a man in his thirties with the same shaggy hair as his pet exploding from beneath a wool knit cap. The man wore a T-shirt and cargo shorts. A leash was wrapped around one hand. Carlos had heard that people sometimes looked like their pets, but he hadn't really believed it until that moment.

"Is this your dog?" Carlos asked.

"Yeah," the man said. "Killer."

At the sound of his name, Killer perked his head up.

"Sorry," Keisha said, standing back up. "We're looking for a lost dog, and well . . ."

"Where did you get that collar?" Hayden asked.

"Ooooh, that thing?" The man nodded. "Yeah, I found that on the sidewalk by a couple of trash barrels."

"Really?" Jaden asked.

"I know, right? A perfectly good collar. Practically new. Killer digs it."

"Where did you find it?" Carlos asked.

"Aw, man, I can't remember." The man thought a minute. "Wait. I went out for some pizza." It suddenly seemed to click. "Yeah, it was right next to Zippy 'Za. Mmmmm, their Meat Explosion pizza is like a slice of heaven."

"Totally," Jaden agreed.

"Zippy 'Za? That's right next to Pets Galore," Carlos said.

He mulled it over. What did it mean? The pieces were starting to shuffle together, but he couldn't see the whole picture.

"Thanks," Carlos said to the man.

"No prob," the man said. Then he slapped his leg. "Come on, Killer. Let's go, bud."

Killer lumbered to his feet and shook his whole body in a wave of motion. He and his owner, like two peas in a pod, wandered off, leaving the Snoops lost and alone in a sea of mutts.

CHAPTER 8

BARK TO SCHOOL

The next day Carlos woke to the smell of breakfast. He dressed and headed downstairs. His mom was already off to work, but his dad was in the kitchen, humming and cooking. Food was his dad's passion. Diaz Groceries had been in their family for half a century. Carlos' grandpa had opened it, and his father had taken it over when Carlos was just a baby.

"*Buenos días*, Carlos," his dad said.

"*Buenos días*, Papa," Carlos replied as he sat at the table. His dad slid a plate of steaming food in front of him — eggs and peppers, fresh avocado, and homemade tortillas. That was the great thing about having a foodie dad: his meals were never boring.

"Tonight is the night of the big basketball game, right?" his dad asked as he quickly cleaned the kitchen.

"Yep." Carlos didn't want to tell his dad about Champ, or the Snoops crew's unsuccessful attempts at finding the missing mutt.

"Should be a great game," his dad said. "Of course, with Ashton Oakley on the court, the Bulldogs are practically guaranteed a win against Watson."

"I guess." Carlos pulled apart his tortilla and began to eat.

His dad plucked an apron off a hook. "I need to hurry down to the store to open. Will you be okay to lock up when you leave?"

Carlos nodded.

"Be good. And have a great day at school."
With that, Carlos' dad whisked out the door, off to
another long day of work.

* * *

"Why does it look like it snowed in front of the
school?" Jaden asked as he crammed a frosted
toaster pastry in his mouth.

Carlos, who'd been daydreaming as the
Snoops walked to school, looked up from the
sidewalk to the school, about a block ahead of
them. In stark contrast to the red-brick building,
the row of trees planted along the sidewalk in
front of the school were coated in white.

"That's not snow," Keisha said. "It's toilet
paper."

Indeed, as the Snoops got closer, they saw
every tree was covered in toilet paper. It hung
from branches, twisted around twigs, and
dangled from leaves. Along with the toilet paper
hung colorful blue and yellow streamers.

"Watson school colors," Carlos said, reaching up and plucking a streamer from the nearest tree.

"So this was their prank?" Jaden asked. "It didn't have anything to do with Champ?"

Hayden had her tablet out, buzzing through the School Ties site. She nodded. "They're bragging about it already," she said. "'Now the Bulldogs will have something to clean up their terrible basketball game tonight.'"

"Guess that takes them off the suspect list," Keisha said.

As they walked into the school, Carlos said, "I wonder why Principal Snider's not outside barking orders to have this mess cleaned up." He only had to wonder for a moment, though. When the quartet rounded the corner by the principal's office, they came upon a stir of activity.

Carlos craned his neck to look out over the hubbub. "Wow, what's going on?"

"Let's find out." Keisha muscled past the crowd forming at the door beside Principal Snider's office.

"Excuse me," Keisha said. She shouldered open the door, and the crowd spilled out into the courtyard.

"Keisha! Carlos!" Polly McDonald was as cheerful as Carlos had ever seen her. Especially considering the school's trees looked like mummies and Principal Snider was probably pretty peeved about that.

"Champ is back!" Polly nearly squealed with delight.

Sure enough, the missing bulldog was in the middle of the courtyard, happily snuggled in Principle Snider's arms. Around Champ's neck was a bright-red collar. Next to Principal Snider was Oliver Noonan, smiling sheepishly.

"Wow!" Keisha was baffled. "Ollie, did you find Champ?"

"He sure did," Principal Snider boomed, clapping Ollie on the shoulder.

"I was walking to school this morning, and I saw him rummaging around a dumpster in the alleyway near my apartment building," Ollie

explained. "I borrowed a leash from a neighbor and caught him."

"I can't believe the nightmare is over." Polly ran over and gave Ollie a big hug. The boy's cheeks flushed red. "And just in time for tonight's game!"

Carlos was super confused about this turn of events, but he held his emotions in check. "Looks like Champ will be able to cheer on the team tonight," he said.

"Looks like it," Ollie said.

"Wonderful!" Principal Snider said. "Oliver, you've saved the day. I cannot thank you enough."

Ollie toed the dirt with one foot. "It's just luck, sir," he said.

"Well, our luck has officially turned," Principal Snider said. "And I have a very good feeling about tonight's game against Watson."

The morning bell rang sharply through the halls and the courtyard.

"Off to class, all," Principal Snider said. He shooed the growing crowd away. Carlos watched as Snider scratched Champ furiously behind the ears, releasing an explosion of tiny dog hairs.

"Good to have you back, little buddy," Snider said. "Now let's go get that mess outside all cleaned up."

Boys and girls, murmuring about Champ's return, walked off to class. Carlos and Keisha joined them. Carlos cast a last look back at Champ.

"Something smells as foul as dog breath about this," he said.

"Why's that?" Keisha asked.

"Because Champ wasn't a bit dirty. If he'd been roaming around the alleys for two days, he should have been covered in filth." He paused. "Also? We found Champ's collar on another dog, remember? But now he's wearing a brand-new collar."

CHAPTER 9

HALFTIME HERO

The rest of the day, Carlos heard other students talking about Oliver's timely rescue of Champ. The common thought was that Polly must have left the gate unlatched after all. Carlos admitted that it was the most likely explanation for Champ's disappearance. Besides, it appeared that neither Frankie nor the Watson basketball team had dognapped the school mascot.

But something about all this didn't sit right with Carlos. If Champ had simply run away and spent the last couple of days roaming the streets, then how had he gotten a brand-new collar?

It seemed the mystery was still . . . well, a mystery.

"Man, this place is packed," Hayden said as she and Jaden joined their friends that evening outside the Fleischman gymnasium. Basketball fans from both teams had been streaming in and filling the bleachers.

"We should find a seat," Jaden suggested. He grabbed his sister's arm and checked her watch. "Tip-off's in twenty minutes."

Keisha led the way to the gymnasium. It was the biggest crowd of the season so far, and people were still arriving. Before long, it would be standing room only.

"Here!" Jaden spied a small length of free bleacher space in the second row on the Fleischman side of the gym. Polly McDonald was seated nearby; she shuffled over to join them.

"How exciting," Polly said. "I'm so glad Champ is back. Otherwise, this game would have been a real downer."

"Where is the little fella?" Hayden asked.

"Principal Snider is going to bring him out as part of the halftime festivities," Polly replied.

"Cool!" Jaden said.

As the teams warmed up on the court, Carlos watched Ashton Oakley drain three-point shots like they were layups. He was good — really good. Oliver was out there, too, practicing a free throw. It clanged high off the rim, and he chased after it.

The Fleischman pep band began to belt out the school fight song. The crowd rose to its feet and clapped along. The spirit squad — along with Chomp, the oversized mascot — jogged onto the court to lead the crowd's cheers.

"Go Bulldogs!" Jaden whooped as the team took the court. Ashton led the charge, standing tallest among players for both basketball teams.

Fleischman's star athlete dominated the first half, taking the ball to the hoop nearly every time he touched it. "He's on fire!" Jaden shouted after the Bulldogs' star sank a three-pointer from the corner. He bumped fists with an old man seated behind them.

Carlos had to admit, Ashton was a dynamic player, despite being a ball hog. Watson, for all their trash-talking and toilet-papering, didn't offer much of a challenge. When the buzzer sounded at the end of the first half, the Bulldogs were up by twelve points. The teams stayed on the sidelines, drinking water and listening to their coaches strategize for the second half. As they did, Frankie Dixon and the rest of the spirit squad jogged to mid-court. The lights dimmed, and music began to pulse through the gym.

"Ladies and gentlemen," Principal Snider said over the loudspeaker. "We here at Fleischman Middle School had quite a scare this week. Our new but already beloved mascot, Champ, found a way to wiggle out of his cage."

Murmurs and soft gasps floated through the bleachers.

"Never fear!" Principal Snider continued. "Champ has been returned to us, thanks to one of our very own Bulldog basketball players! Champ! Ollie! Come on out!"

Oliver Noonan walked from the end of the bench out to center court as the music swelled. The spirit squad rallied around him as Frankie Dixon brought a wild and happy Champ out to join them.

"Let's hear it for Ollie and Champ!"

The crowd burst into applause. Some stood. Others whistled and waved. At center court, Ollie waved back. His smile was a mile wide.

The rest of the basketball team came out onto the court to warm up for the second half as Champ was led to the sidelines. Some of the players stooped to scratch the bulldog behind the ear. Champ leaped up on their legs, tongue wagging, to oblige. Others huddled around Ollie, slapping high fives and making jokes.

"That should be us out there," Jaden muttered so quietly Carlos could barely hear it. Yeah, maybe Jaden was right. It stung just a bit that Snoops, Inc., didn't find Champ and solve the mystery. But in the end, Champ was safe, and that was what mattered.

Ashton Oakley, ball tucked under one arm, was one of the last to jog out. As he passed Champ, the dog ran over and brushed up against the star athlete's leg. Ashton didn't

return the love; he continued on out and put up a jump shot that hit nothing but nylon.

Carlos watched as Ashton raced for his own rebound, came to a stop, and sneezed. Once. Twice. And then a third time.

"Huh, that's interesting," Carlos said. He couldn't take his eyes off Ashton.

"What's up?" Keisha asked.

"I think I figured out what happened to Champ," he said with a smile.

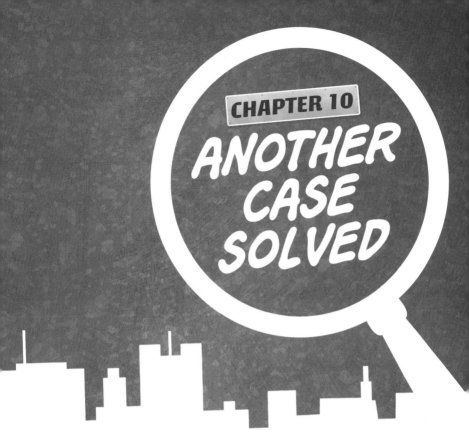

CHAPTER 10

ANOTHER CASE SOLVED

"Whoa," Jaden said after Carlos had filled the other Snoops and Polly in on his thoughts. They were all huddled together in the bleachers while the second half of the game began on the court in front of them.

"So I didn't leave the cage unlatched?" Polly asked, relief in her voice.

Carlos shook his head. "You didn't."

"How sure are you about this?" Keisha asked.

"Pretty sure. I just have to make a phone call."

The second half of the basketball game picked up right where the first half left off. The Bulldogs owned the court. With about two minutes left in the game, Carlos excused himself to make his phone call. "I'll meet you guys outside the school after the game," he said.

"Good luck," Hayden said.

"Thanks."

Carlos made his way to the boys' locker room. Once there, he called Pets Galore and spoke to Trina, who gave him the information he'd hoped for. "I knew it," he said after hanging up.

Carlos waited in the locker room. He could hear the frenzied crowd as the Bulldogs brought home a big victory. The band played the team off the court. Soon, the players came busting into the locker room, sweaty and excited.

"Great win, guys!" Carlos said, high-fiving some of the players who didn't seem to care that he was hanging out in the locker room.

But Ashton Oakley gave him a peculiar look. "What are you doing in here?" he asked.

Carlos shrugged. "I just need to talk."

"To who?"

Carlos plopped down on a wooden bench near Oliver Noonan. "This guy," he said, nodding his head at the benchwarmer.

"Me?" Oliver said with a puzzled look. Carlos noticed that Ollie's jersey, unlike most of the team's, was not soaked in sweat. That meant he probably didn't even play, and it was the biggest game of the season.

Carlos waited until the players closest to them had changed and filtered out of the locker room before quietly asking, "So . . . why did you do it?"

"Do what?" Ollie was acting befuddled, but Carlos had seen fake confusion before.

"Why did you take Champ?"

Ollie snorted and laughed. "*Take* Champ? I *found* Champ, Carlos."

"Sure, you found him," Carlos said, "after two days alone in the city, clean and wearing a

brand-new collar. I know it's new because we found his old one last night on a shaggy dog at Ruff Patch Dog Park. I phoned Trina over at Pets Galore. She told me she sold a new collar to a boy matching your description two nights ago, along with a few other doggie treats and toys."

Ollie shook his head, but he began to change out of his sneakers a little quicker. His hands were shaking. "I'm a hero," Ollie said. "Not a thief. I don't know what you're talking about."

"Okay." Carlos reached down and grabbed Ollie's coat that he had tossed onto his duffle bag.

"Wait, what are you doing?" Ollie asked. "Give that back."

"Hey, Ashton," Carlos said. The star athlete stood by the locker room door, chatting it up with a couple of other players.

"What?" Ashton asked.

"Catch." Carlos tossed Ollie's coat in a high arc across the locker room. Ashton snatched it out of the air.

"Why are you giving me Noonan's jack — ack — AH-CHOO!"

Ashton's sneeze echoed across the locker room. The players nearest him jumped back.

"*Gesundheit*," Carlos said smugly. "Allergies, right?"

"Yeah," Ashton said. He threw the coat back to Carlos. "So what?"

"That's why you were gung-ho about Chomp and didn't want Champ as the team mascot. You sneeze when you're around the real bulldog."

"Yeah, sure, I guess." Ashton turned his back on Carlos and continued his conversation.

Carlos looked closely at Ollie's coat and saw a large amount of dog hair stuck to it, the same kind that he and Keisha found on the pillow in Champ's kennel. "When Jaden and I were asking questions at practice, Ashton moved your coat. It had dog hair and dander all over it, didn't it? So let me ask you again, why'd you do it?"

Ollie looked over at Ashton and the remaining players, who were making their way out of the locker room. When it was just he and Carlos left, Ollie said, "I sit next to Ashton on the bench every day, but I never get to play. He gets all the glory, and I get a prime seat to watch. Some guys, well, they just don't get to be the hero."

"So you dognapped Champ?"

"I always meant to bring him back. I knew that if I did, people would stop looking at Ashton for a little while and look at me instead." He sighed. "So I ditched Champ's collar when I realized there was an app to track it and bought a new one so it wouldn't look suspicious when I brought him back."

Ollie stood and gathered his things into his duffel bag. Then, with slumped shoulders, he said, "Okay. If you're going to bust me, that's fine. Let's go talk to Principal Snider."

Carlos shook his head. "Nah. I'm not gonna bust you, dude."

"You're not?"

"Nope. Champ's safe, and Principal Snider's got his dog back." Carlos stood. "Look, I know how you feel, Ollie. But you wanna know a secret? We all feel that way sometimes. Like we'll never be the hero. But we will. We just have to find what makes us each heroic. So no, Principal Snider doesn't need to know what's what. But only if you agree to one thing."

"What's that?"

"Join me and the rest of Snoops, Inc., for pizza. We're going to Zippy 'Za."

A smile danced on Ollie's lips. He nodded. "Yeah," he said. "That sounds like fun."

The two boys exited the locker room and walked out of the school. Keisha, Hayden, Jaden, and Polly McDonald sat on the cement steps waiting for them.

When they saw Carlos and Ollie, the team jumped to their feet.

"Everything cool?" Keisha asked.

Carlos nodded. "Yep."

"Gonna fill us in on the details?"

Carlos slipped an arm around Ollie's shoulder. They began to walk down the sidewalk. "Sure am . . . over an extra-large Meat Explosion pizza."

"Now that's what I'm talking about," Jaden said. The rest of the Snoops laughed.

The friends walked down the sidewalk together, another case solved by Snoops, Incorporated.

THE END

▮ Snoops, Inc. Case Report #001

Prepared by Carlos Diaz

THE CASE:

Track down and find Fleischman Middle School's missing mascot, Champ the bulldog.

CRACKING THE CASE:

This mystery sure was a tricky one, because we didn't know if Champ just got loose, or if someone had snatched him. Thankfully, Hayden helped us track down an important clue using GPS, or the Global Positioning System.

So, GPS is a system of two-dozen satellites that work together to create a grid-like map of Earth. The map uses a special numerical code to accurately pinpoint a location anywhere on the planet. Things like phones and some computers have GPS receivers in them. They connect with the satellites to show exactly where you are.

GPS is helpful when you're lost or need to map out a route from one place to another. Even boats and planes use GPS receivers so they won't get lost – no matter what the weather is like. Pretty cool stuff.

Unfortunately, the PetTracker3000 technology from Champ's TechPet dog collar didn't lead us directly to him. But, it did lead to a big clue that made it a whole lot easier for us to . . .

CRACK THE CASE!▬

WHAT DO YOU THINK?

1. Carlos is the unofficial leader of Snoops, Incorporated. What qualities do you think he has that make him qualified for this position?

2. Each member of Snoops, Incorporated, seems to have a particular talent. How do their talents help them work together as a team? What skills or talents would you bring to the team?

3. Ollie's motive for dognapping Champ was the desire to be a hero. Have you ever felt like this before? Why?

WRITE YOUR OWN!

1. Pretend you're the leader of your own detective agency. Write an advertisement for your agency and the types of mysteries you wish to solve.

2. Agatha the cat hangs around Snoops HQ all the time. Write a short story from her point of view and how she sees each of the four detectives.

3. Pretend that you are Oliver Noonan, and you've just confessed to dognapping Champ. Write a letter to Principal Snider apologizing for the act. Include your reasoning for making such a drastic choice.

GLOSSARY

ACNE (AK-nee)—a condition caused by blocked oil glands in the skin that results in swollen red pimples

ALLERGIC (uh-LUHR-jik)—when someone is sensitive to something that causes them to sneeze, have a rash, or feel sick

ASPHALT (AS-fawlt)—a black tar that is mixed with sand and gravel to make paved roads

BEACON (BEE-kuhn)—a light or fire used as a signal or warning

DANDER (DAN-duhr)—tiny scales from hair, feathers, or skin that can cause allergies

MICROCHIP (MYE-kroh-chip)—a tiny circuit that processes information in a computer

PEDESTRIAN (puh-DESS-tree-uhn)—someone who travels on foot

SIDLE (SY-duhl)—to move close to someone in a quiet or secret way

ABOUT THE AUTHOR

Brandon Terrell has been a lifelong fan of mysteries, shown by his collection of nearly 200 Hardy Boys books. He is the author of numerous children's books, including several titles in series such as Tony Hawk's 900 Revolution, Jake Maddox Graphic Novels, Spine Shivers, and Sports Illustrated Kids: Time Machine Magazine.

When not hunched over his laptop, Brandon enjoys watching movies and television, reading, watching and playing baseball, and spending time at home with his wife and two children in Minnesota.

ABOUT THE ILLUSTRATOR

Mariano Epelbaum is an experienced character designer, illustrator, and traditional 2D animator. He has been working as a professional artist since 1996, and enjoys trying different art styles and techniques. Throughout his career Mariano has created many expressive characters and designs for a wide range of films, TV series, commercials, and publications in his native country of Argentina. In addition to Snoops, Inc., Mariano has also contributed to the Fairy Tale Mixups and You Choose: Fractured Fairy Tales series for Capstone.

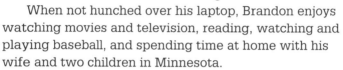

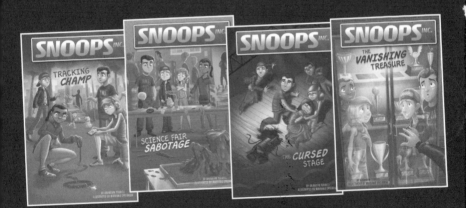